Alfred and the Moonatics

by Kate Street

from

one small step one giant leap

Wonderfully Wearable Shoes

Telephone +44 (0) 20 8740 4045
www.onesmallsteponegiantleap.com

Written by Kate Street, edited by Claire Black
From an original concept by Martin Knox and Lee Keetley
Illustrations by Helen and Thom White
www.mknox.co.uk

First published in Great Britain for one small step one giant leap limited, by Dean
an imprint of Egmont UK Limited, The Yellow Building, 1 Nicholas Road, London W11 4AN

Alfred the Astronaut loved going into space because he always liked to see his special animal friends that lived on the Moon.

Alfred had eight friends. There was a cat called Cleo, a bear called Brutus, a pig called Parker, an owl called Otis, a dog called Duke, a rabbit called Rosie, a duck called Dolly and a little mouse called Matilda.

Alfred called them the Moonatics and they loved it when he came to visit them. He told them fantastic stories about life on Earth.

One day, Alfred was telling the Moonatics about one of his favourite Earthling treats – ice cream.

"Ice cream is very cold and sometimes, when you eat it, you feel like your brain is going to freeze," he said.

"That's how we feel every morning when we leave the Moonatic house and go outside onto the surface of the Moon," squawked Otis.

"Ah," said Alfred. "But the good thing about ice cream is that it's so yummy you soon forget how cold it is. Nearly everyone on Earth likes to eat ice cream. Especially children."

"The best thing about ice cream," Alfred continued, "is that it comes in lots of yummy flavours. My favourite is chocolate."

"What's chocolate?" asked Cleo. She was a curious cat who wanted to know everything about everything.

"Chocolate is brown and smooth and soft as velvet," said Alfred.

"Sounds like me!" boomed Brutus the Bear.

"Don't you mean loud and large?" cackled Cleo.

Matilda squeaked excitedly. "What other flavours are there? Is there cheese flavour? I love cheese."

"No cheese flavour, I'm afraid," giggled Alfred. "But you might like vanilla. It's soft and creamy and the colour of spun gold."

"Mmm! Sounds like cheese to me!" said Matilda, jumping up and down.

"What other flavours are there?" the rest of the Moonatics asked.

"Well, let's see," said Alfred. "There's strawberry. It's pink and sweet."

"Sounds like me!" honked Parker the Pig.

Cleo laughed. "Pink and sweet? You mean stinky, silly and slow."

All the Moonatics laughed apart from Rosie the Rabbit.

"None of the ice cream flavours sound like me," she said, sadly.

"Oh no," Alfred replied. "There's one that's perfect for you, Rosie. It's called marshmallow and it has bouncy pillows of fluff that dance in your mouth when you eat it."

Rosie sighed. "Oh wow. I wish I could go to Earth and try some!"

Soon, all the Moonatics were jumping up and down
with excitement.

"I want to try chocolate!"

"And vanilla!"

"Strawberry for me!"

"We all want to go to Earth and eat ice cream!"

Alfred had an idea. "Why don't I take you there?" he asked.
"We could go in my space ship."

The Moonatics cheered. "Yes please, Alfred! We've never
left the Moon before."

VANiLLa

chOCOLate

strawberry

broCColi

caBBage

Alfred fired up the engines and the rocket started to shake. The Moonatics huddled together.

"I'm scared," whimpered Brutus.

"You're a big strong bear, you don't need to be afraid," snorted Parker.

"I'm hungry," said a little voice.

"You're always hungry, Matilda," said Cleo, swishing her tail.

"Prepare for Lift Off!" shouted Alfred. "Moonatics, help me countdown."

"10, 9, 8, 7, 6, 5, 4, 3, 2, 1 ..."

The rocket blasted into space.

The Moonatics gazed out of the window. They could see little stars twinkling against the night sky and below them something that looked like a small, round cheese.

The cheese seemed to be getting nearer and nearer and bigger and bigger.

"Are we going to land on a piece of Stilton?" asked Matilda, her whiskers twitching in excitement. "Mmm, Stilton. I love cheese!"

Matilda may have been the smallest Moonatic but she had the biggest appetite, especially where cheese was concerned!

Alfred laughed. "It's not cheese, it's Earth and we're due to land there any second now. HOLD ON TIGHT!"

They landed with a BUMP!

"Now then," said Alfred, looking out of the window. "Where on Earth are we?"

A red double decker bus sailed past. Then another. And another.

"I know where we are!" Alfred shouted. "This is England. We're in London."

The Moonatics climbed out of the spaceship. They couldn't believe their eyes. They had never seen so many people and buildings.

"Oh dear," said Brutus, peeping out of the door. "It's very busy. I think I want to go home."

"Don't be scared," said Matilda, gently. "If we stick together we'll be okay. Let's explore!"

They saw a river and a big wheel, and then a beautiful palace.

"That's where the Queen lives," Alfred told them. "She's the head of the country," he explained.

"So I'm the Queen of the Moon," nodded Brutus, who liked to think he was the head of the Moonatics because he was the biggest.

"A queen is a girl," Alfred chuckled, "so you would be King of the Moon, Brutus."

"Moon King!" boomed Brutus. "I like that."

"I could be a king too!" barked Duke the Dog. "Bark-king."

"I could be a king too! Quack-king," quacked Dolly.

"And me," said Matilda. "I would be Squeak-king."

"And I would be Oink-king," said Parker.

"I hope you're all just jo-king," purred Cleo. "Everyone knows that I am Queen of the Moonatics."

The Moonatics explored all afternoon. They learnt many things about the people who lived in London.

Curious Cleo the Cat wanted to know why so many of the Earthlings travelled around in metal boxes with wheels.

"These are called cars," said Alfred. "Humans travel around in them because they only have two legs and they can't move very fast."

Otis the Owl looked at the traffic jam that stretched all the way along the street. "I don't think much of these cars," he said. "Walking would be much quicker."

Otis was right as usual.

The Moonatics started to get tired.

"We need to find somewhere safe to stay for the night," said Alfred.

The clouds grew darker and darker and the Moonatics felt drops of water falling from the sky.

Rosie started to cry. "Oh dear. The Moon is missing us," she wept.

"Why do you think that, Rosie?" asked Duke.

"Because he's crying," she replied. "Look. His tears are making the pavement all wet."

"The Moon isn't sad, Rosie," said Alfred. "It's just rain. The clouds are watering the earth so that the plants and flowers can grow."

"I love the rain!" exclaimed Dolly Duck. "I've taken to it like a duck to water!"

"You are a duck, Dolly..." groaned Cleo.

The rain poured down and soon everyone was wet and miserable.

Then they came to a parade of shops.

"Look!" said Alfred, with a beaming smile across his face. "It's a sign!"

Indeed it was a sign that hung above the shop. It read:

"One Small Step One Giant Leap."

"I can't believe it!" shouted Alfred. "That's just like the first words spoken on the Moon."

The Moonatics cheered.

Alfred looked through the window. "It's a shoe shop," he said.

In the window the Moonatics could see shoes of every colour and shape from teeny weenie to junior astronaut size.

"What are shoes?" asked Cleo.

"Earthlings wear shoes on their feet to protect them and make them look nice," Alfred explained. "This must be a shoe shop for children because some of the shoes are very small."

"I wish I could have some new shoes," said Rosie.

"I don't think they make them tiny enough for rabbits," said Alfred, stroking Rosie's ears.

The Moonatics ran inside the shop to hide. Poor Brutus had trouble fitting underneath a low wooden bench, and his feet poked out of the end.

A boy in a blue apron came over and pointed at the pair of furry feet.

"Your son looks like he has quite a pair on him!" he said to Alfred with a smile. "Would you like me to measure him?"

He's not my son, he's a bear, thought Alfred. And you'll get a bit of a shock if you try to measure his feet.

"Erm, we're just looking at the moment, thank you," said Alfred.

"Ok," said the boy, disappearing into the back of the shop, "but we're closing in a couple of minutes."

"I'm going to find some food for our supper," whispered Alfred to the Moonatics. "Stay here until I come back."

"Don't forget the ice cream!" squeaked Matilda.

Shortly after Alfred left, the boy in the apron turned off all the lights, left the shop and locked the door.

All was quiet in the One Small Step One Giant Leap shoe shop. The Moonatics realised they were alone.

They leapt out from under the bench.

"Let's play hide and seek until Alfred comes back!" yapped Duke the Dog.

And so they did.

Brutus, Cleo, Duke, Rosie, Otis, Dolly, Parker and little Matilda all chose a place to hide. Next time you come to the shoe shop, see if you can find them!

one small step one giant leap

Wonderfully Wearable Shoes
Telephone +44 (0) 20 8740 4045
www.onesmallsteponegiantleap.com

Bath
6 Cheap Street, Bath,
Avon BA1 1NE

Dublin: House of Fraser
Children's Department, House Of Fraser,
Dundrum Shopping Centre,
Sandyford Road, Dublin 16

Kingston: Bentalls
Bentalls, Wood Street,
Kingston upon Thames,
Surrey, KT1 1TX

London: Clapham
49 Northcote Road, Clapham,
London SW11 1NJ

London: Islington
46 Cross Street, Islington,
London N1 2BA

London: Notting Hill
3 Blenheim Crescent, Notting Hill,
London W11 2EE

London: Putney
Unit D2, The Exchange,

Putney High Street, London SW15 1TW

London: Ealing
4 The Green, Ealing,
London W5 5DA

London: East Sheen
409 Upper Richmond Road West,
East Sheen, London SW14 7NX

London: Harrods
87 - 135 Brompton Road, Knightsbridge,
London SW1X 7XL

Manchester: House of Fraser
Childrenswear Department,
House Of Fraser, 98 - 116 Deansgate,
Manchester M3 2QG

Teddington
32 High Street, Teddington,
Middlesex TW11 8EW

Windsor: Daniel
121 - 125 Peascod Street, Windsor,
Berkshire SL4 1DP

the
h&ven

Breast Cancer Support Centres

We support the wonderful work of The Haven. So, if you have enjoyed this free
book, please donate generously. Visit: http://www.thehaven.org.uk